Dear Parent,

What's that noise? Frog's so scared that he hops out of bed and straight to his friend's house. Duck is brave and comforting—until he starts hearing things too. And Pig can't calm the two of them down without getting silly himself. So, how will the friends make it through till morning?

With the simplest of text and brightly colored illustrations, author-artist Max Velthuijs manages to be both comforting and encouraging as he explores, with great accuracy, the emotions and perspectives of children who imagine monsters in the night.

We hope you and your child enjoy this tale of Frog and his friends.

Sincerely,

Fritz J. Luecke

Fritz J. Luecke
Editorial Director
Weekly Reader Books

Weekly Reader Children's Book Club Presents

Frog Is Frightened

Max Velthuijs

Tambourine Books  New York

This book is a presentation of Newfield Publications, Inc.
For information about Newfield Publications book clubs for children write to:
Newfield Publications, Inc.,
4343 Equity Drive, Columbus, Ohio 43228

Published by arrangement with Tambourine Books, a division of William Morrow & Company, Inc.
Newfield Publications is a federally registered trademark of Newfield Publications, Inc.
Weekly Reader is a federally registered trademark of Weekly Reader Corporation.

1996 edition

Copyright © 1994 by Max Velthuijs
First Published in Great Britain by Andersen Press Ltd.

LIBRARY OF CONGRESS CATALOGING IN PUBLICATION DATA
Velthuijs, Max, 1923-
Frog is Frightened / by Max Velthuijs. — 1st U.S. ed. p. cm.
Summary: Strange noises in the night frighten Frog and his animal friends.
[1. Fear of the dark—Fiction. 2. Frog—Fiction. 3. Animals—Fiction.] I. Title.
PZ7.V5Fu 1995 [E]—dc20 94-24596 CIP AC
ISBN 0-688-14203-6

Frog was very frightened. He was lying in bed, and he heard strange noises everywhere. There was a creaking in the cupboard and a rustling under the floorboards.

Somebody's under my bed, thought Frog.

He jumped out of bed and ran through the dark woods until he reached Duck's house.

"How nice of you to drop by," said Duck. "But it's very late. I'm about to go to bed."

"Please, Duck," said Frog. "I'm scared. There's a ghost under my bed."

"Nonsense," laughed Duck. "There aren't any ghosts."

"There are so," said Frog. "The woods are haunted too."

"Don't be frightened," said Duck. "You can stay with me. I'm not scared."

And they huddled into bed together. Frog cuddled close and wasn't frightened any more.

All of a sudden they heard a scratching noise on the roof.
"What was that?" asked Duck, sitting up with a jolt.
The next moment they heard a creaking on the stairs.
"This house is haunted too!" shouted Frog. "Let's get out of here."
And they ran out into the woods.

Frog and Duck ran as fast as they could.

They were sure there were ghosts and monsters everywhere.

Eventually they reached Pig's house, and, gasping for breath, they hammered on the door.

"Who is it?" asked a sleepy voice.

"Please, Pig, open the door. It's us," shouted Frog and Duck.

"What's the matter?" grumbled Pig. "Why have you woken me up in the middle of the night?"

"Please help us," said Duck. "The woods are full of ghosts and monsters."

Pig laughed. "What nonsense. Ghosts and monsters don't exist. You know that."

"Well, look for yourself," said Frog.

Pig looked out the window, but he couldn't see anything unusual.

"Please, Pig, may we stay here? We're so scared."

"Okay," said Pig. "My bed's big enough. And I'm never frightened by all that rubbish."

So there they were, all three of them together in Pig's bed.
"This is nice," said Frog. "Nothing can happen now."
But they couldn't sleep. They listened to all the strange,
frightening noises in the woods. This time, Pig heard them too!

But luckily the three friends had each other. They shouted out that they weren't scared—that they weren't afraid of anything. Eventually they fell asleep, exhausted.

Next morning, Hare went to visit Frog. The door was wide open, but Frog was nowhere to be seen.

This is strange, thought Hare.

Duck's house was empty too.

"Duck, Duck, where are you?" shouted Hare. But there was no answer. Hare was very worried. He thought something terrible must have happened.

Terrified, he ran through the woods looking for Frog and Duck. He looked and looked, but there was no trace of his friends. Maybe Pig will know where they are, he thought.

Hare knocked on Pig's door. There was no answer. It was very quiet. He looked in through the window, and there he saw his friends fast asleep. It was almost lunchtime! Hare knocked on the window.

"Help! A ghost!" shouted Frog and Pig and Duck.
Then they saw that it was Hare.

Pig unlocked the door, and they all ran outside.

"Oh, Hare," they said, "we were so frightened. The woods are full of ghosts and scary monsters."

"Ghosts and monsters?" said Hare. "There's no such thing."

"How do you know?" said Frog angrily. "There was one under my bed."

"Did you see it?" asked Hare.

"Well, no," said Frog.

Frog, Duck, and Pig all talked at once about scary noises in the night.

Finally, Pig made some breakfast.
"You know," said Hare, "Everyone gets frightened sometimes."
"Even you?" asked Frog.

"Oh, yes," said Hare. "I was very frightened this morning when I thought something happened to you."
There was a silence.

Then everyone laughed.
"Don't be silly, Hare," said Frog. "You have nothing to fear.
We'll always be here."